Binch, Caroline.
The silver shoes.

$15.95

DATE			

For Amy and
Kingfisher Blue

DK

LONDON, NEW YORK, SYDNEY, DELHI, PARIS,
MUNICH, and JOHANNESBURG

First American Edition, 2001

Published in the United States by
DK Publishing, Inc.
95 Madison Avenue
New York, New York 10016

01 02 03 04 05 10 9 8 7 6 5 4 3 2 1
Text and illustrations copyright © 2001 Caroline Binch

Library of Congress Cataloging-in-Publication Data
Binch, Caroline
The silver shoes / written and illustrated by Caroline Binch - 1st American ed.
p. cm.
Summary: A young girl starting dance classes wants silver shoes like her grandmother's, but when told she must
wait to see if she likes the class first, she finds a noisy, used pair of shoes to wear in the meantime.
ISBN 0-7894-7905-2
[I. Dance - Fiction. 2. Shoes - Fiction. 3. Racially mixed people - Fiction.] I. Title.
PZ7. B5116 Sg 2001   [E] - dc21   2001028497

Color reproduction by Dot Gradations, UK. Printed and bound in Italy by L.E.G.O.

See our complete
catalog at
www.dk.com

Silver Shoes

written and illustrated by Caroline Binch

DK Publishing, Inc.

Gran's bottom drawer seemed like a treasure chest to Molly. Inside were sparkly bags, shiny shoes, and brightly colored shawls. Beautiful things for Gran to wear when she went dancing with Grandad.

"Can I wear your silver shoes, Gran?" Molly always asked.
Clickety-clackety went the heels as Molly danced.
She felt just like a grown-up lady.

At home Molly danced with her best friend Beverly.
They liked to dress up and copy the stars on television.
"Girls, I think it's time you went to dancing lessons,"
laughed Molly's mom.
"Can I have some silver shoes?" asked Molly. "Just like Gran's."
But Molly's mom said she had to wait to see if she liked the
classes before they bought any shoes.

For the dance class Molly and Beverly wore their prettiest dresses. "Hello, I'm Mrs. Clover," said the teacher. "Welcome to our dance class." Molly looked at the teacher's shoes. They were silver. She looked around the hall. Nearly all the other girls had silver shoes, too.

"Mrs. Clover, I don't have any silver shoes,"
said Molly in dismay.
"That's okay," said the teacher, smiling.
"But my Gran has silver shoes for
dancing," said Molly in a wobbly voice.
She buried her head in her mom's dress.
"Mommy, I want to go home."

The following week, Beverly ran into Molly's house
holding a pair of shoes — silver shoes.
"Look what I have!" she shouted.

Beverly had been given an old pair of silver shoes that her cousin
had outgrown. Molly didn't want to play with her friend anymore.
But Mom had an idea.

At the thrift shop, they found a blouse for Mom, two jigsaw puzzles, and some toys for Steven, but no silver shoes for Molly.

Then Molly saw them. A beautiful pair of silver shoes almost exactly the same as Gran's.

"Mommy, look, I found them!" she shrieked.

"Those are adult shoes, Molly," said Mom. "You won't be able to dance in them." But Molly wanted them anyway.

Molly kept the silver shoes by her bed that night. As soon as she woke up, she put them on and she wore them all day long. She couldn't wait to show them to Gran.

Together they twirled
around Gran's tiny living room
until they were dizzy.

On Tuesday, Molly and Beverly went to dance class again.
"Look, Mrs. Clover, I have my silver shoes now. They are just like
my Gran's and she does real dancing," said Molly proudly.

But Mrs. Clover shook her head.

"I'm sorry, Molly, high heels won't do," she said kindly.

"You might trip and hurt yourself. Please, wear your ordinary shoes."

Daddy came home early that evening.
"Let's go to the park," he suggested.
"You can ride your bike, Molly."
"Yippee!" Molly cried. "I'll wear
my silver shoes."
Daddy looked at Mommy.
"Why don't you wear your other shoes
to ride your bike, Molly? You can
put the silver shoes in the basket."

Daddy pushed Molly
and Steven high on
the swings and
bought them both
ice cream.

They had such a good time
that Molly forgot all about
her silver shoes
until bedtime.

Molly snuggled under the covers as Daddy tucked her in.
"I'd really like some real silver shoes," she sighed.
"Now, Molly, I'll tell you a secret," whispered Dad. "Special
things that you want very much often come at special times."
"But I may have to wait ages for a special time," said Molly.
"Plenty of time, pumpkin, to learn some new dances with
Mrs. Clover," replied Dad.
Molly smiled sleepily and hugged her daddy goodnight.

At dance class the next week, Molly was concentrating so hard she forgot she was wearing ordinary shoes. The following week, Molly had such fun she didn't think about her shoes at all.

And in the third week, she danced so fast she could hardly see her feet!

In the fourth week, it was Molly's birthday. She tore open her presents one by one. She saved Gran and Grandad's present until last.
"Silver shoes! My own silver shoes!" cried Molly happily, and she put them on.

Now Molly felt like
a real dancer.

But she still liked to wear her clickety-clackety shoes when she danced for Gran.